Waldo, Tell Me About Christmas

The C. R. Gibson Company, Norwalk, CT 06856

ISBN 0-8378-1846-X

GB345

Waldo, Tell Me About Christmas

by Hans Wilhelm

The C.R. Gibson Company
Norwalk, CT 06856

Michael counted the days on his calendar. Then he got worried.

"Christmas is almost here," he cried, "and we have no gifts, no decorations and no fancy food."

His best friend Waldo came into the
room.
    "Waldo," said Michael, "we're not
ready for Christmas." Waldo smiled.

"Would you like to take a sleigh ride into the forest with me?" asked Waldo.

"All right," said Michael, "but when we get back we have to start getting ready for Christmas."

Michael put on his jacket and his cap. Then he got his sleigh and the two friends left home for the forest.

It was a lovely day. The air was fresh and crisp. The trees sparkled with snow.

"Waldo," said Michael, "it won't be Christmas if I don't buy presents. I have to buy a lot—for Mom, for Dad, for Granny and Grandpa, for my friends and of course for you. I wonder what I should get for you for Christmas, Waldo."

Waldo didn't answer. He smiled as they entered the forest.

It was very quiet, but Michael didn't seem to notice.

"And if we don't have decorations we won't have Christmas. We need a big tree with lots of things on it. And wreaths and candles and all that stuff."

Waldo was silent.

"And we have to have a feast!" continued Michael. "Maybe we can find a goose or a turkey or something." Waldo remained silent.

Then Michael asked, "What are you doing, Waldo?"

"I'm putting out some food for the animals. You can help me if you like," Waldo answered.

Michael got up from the sleigh to help Waldo. "And if I don't get a lot of presents it won't be Christmas," he said. "I'd better make my list for Santa Claus when we get home. Presents are the best part of Christmas."

"Maybe for some people," said Waldo quietly. "But that is not Christmas. Christmas is something very different."

"What do you mean?" asked Michael.

"Come sit down beside me
on the sleigh," said Waldo.
"I'll tell you about Christmas."

Michael snuggled close to his
friend and listened.

"It was a long time ago," began Waldo, "but the world was not much different than it is today. There was a lot of sadness everywhere. Many people had turned away from God and lived very selfish lives.

"Some were jealous, greedy, angry and always fighting with each other. No one seemed to be very happy.

"But God, our Father, loved His children very much. He had sent many wise people to teach His children how to be happy and live in peace, but only a few listened and learned and changed their ways.

"Finally God decided to send His very own son, Christ, to earth. He would be God's gift of love to all the people in the world. He would teach God's children.

"It all happened one night in a small town called Bethlehem. The first sign of His arrival was a very bright star which could be seen from far away. On the hills nearby were shepherds sitting around a warm fire. Suddenly the sky opened and bright light filled the air. The shepherds were very scared.

"'Don't be afraid!' said a voice. The shepherds now saw that the light was filled with countless angels. One of the angels spoke and said that this night was one of great joy for everyone. The son of God had been born into the world as a little baby. He could be found in a stable near the town of Bethlehem.

"The shepherds were very surprised and eager to see this child, who was the son of God. They went quickly to look for Him.

"In the stable the shepherds found the little Christ child lying in a manger. They knelt and prayed and thanked God for His gift of love. Then the shepherds went into the streets of Bethlehem and told everyone they met that God's son was born."

"And that was the first Christmas," smiled Waldo. " There were no decorations. There was no Santa Claus. There was no Christmas tree and there was no feast. No animals had to die. It was a time of peace and joy. The gift of love was from God."

Now it was Michael who was silent.
After a while he asked, "Why do we
celebrate Christmas?"

"We celebrate Christmas to give thanks for Christ who came to earth and lives with us in spirit today.

Each Christmas we are reminded of what God wants for us: To be unselfish, to live in harmony with all living creatures and to love God, our Father.

And just as the shepherds shared the good news of Christ's birth with others, so do we share His love with others."

Waldo lifted Michael to his
shoulders.

"Look," he said. "See the first stars
of the night."

Michael gazed at the heavens.
"Maybe this year our Christmas can
be like the shepherds'." He hugged
Waldo.

"I hope so," said Waldo, softly.